W9-DEX-692

Monsters One to Ten

By Emily Thompson
Illustrated by Tom Leigh

Level **Pre 1** Reader

READING LEVEL

® Dalmatian Press, LLC, 2012. All rights reserved.
Published by Dalmatian Press, LLC, 2012. The DALMATIAN PRESS name and logo are trademarks of Dalmatian Press, LLC, Franklin, Tennessee 37067. No part of this book may be reproduced or copied in any form without written permission from the copyright owner.

Printed in China
CE15074/0000/0000

One tire...

...makes a fun swing.

Two hands…

...make a yummy lunch.

Three snowballs…

...make a cold snowman.

Four letters…

...make Elmo's name.

Five music makers...

...make a jazzy band.

Six friends make a tall tower.

Seven stars make
the Big Dipper.

Eight patches...

…make a comfy quilt.

Nine players make
a baseball team.

Ten monsters…

...make a big mess!